Hey Dad!

Let's Have a Catch

by

Harold Theurer, Jr.

illustrations by William Baxter Bledsoe

I was born in Brooklyn, New York at a time when video games hadn't been invented. The only cards we traded were baseball cards and one of the best toys every boy had was a pink, rubber ball. I loved playing catch with my friends or throwing it against the wall, but there was always something special about playing catch with my Dad.

Dad worked two different jobs, one during the day and one at night. I rarely saw him during the week, but it didn't bother me. Each afternoon I would wait for him to come home for dinner, shower and take a quick nap before he went to his night job.

Before he began climbing the steps to the front of the building, I would ask him, "Five minute catch, Dad?" He rarely said, "No" and the five minutes often became fifteen. Unfortunately, then he couldn't take that nap.

In the beginning, I wasn't always a good catcher or thrower. We would stand close together and his throws were soft and right into my hands. Sometimes I would catch them and more often I would drop them. "That's it! You caught it!" or "Keep trying. You'll get it!" he'd say.

My throws weren't so straight. Often they would spin and bounce away from Dad. I'd look in horror as my pink, rubber ball scurried across the street toward the black hole of no return better known as the corner sewer mouth. Dad would rescue the ball from its watery cave. He didn't seem to mind.

As my catching and throwing improved, the pink, rubber ball was replaced by a baseball and glove. I'll always remember the smell of the new, rawhide glove and the oil we used to soften it. As the years went by we didn't stand as close together. When I became more comfortable with the glove I asked, "Throw them high in the air, Dad." And he did.

When the ball stopped in the air at the top of its arc and began its descent Dad would say, "Get under it! Get under it!" If I did and the ball "snapped" into my glove I would hear those magic words, "Nice catch". I hope the smile I wore was as big as the one on his face, a result of not having to run after bad throws. Aside from the sound of the ball snapping in our gloves all one would hear is, "Nice catch." or "Good throw."

These five minute conversations and "catch phrases" were the most memorable because we had them when he really didn't have time to spare.

He may not have been around as much as my friends' dads who might have worked one job, but I always knew he was there for me. I could always dream about the next "catch" we would have together.

As I grew older we didn't have as many catches. Yet, every once in a while I would pick up the ball in the yard and throw it to him, just for fun. A half hour later we'd stop, just like old times, but "Nice catch", "Good throw" weren't necessary. The throws spoke volumes, much like the smile on his face.

July 9, 1990 was Dad's 73rd birthday. We had a barbecue, sang Happy Birthday and cut the cake. When Mom and my wife, went inside, I picked up a tennis ball and the two of us started tossing it back and forth. This time I didn't throw it as hard and made sure he didn't have to run after it. No words were spoken, just the rhythm of the catches and throws of the ball. We stood much closer and I still have memories of this, our last catch.

Five years later I became a dad. I couldn't wait for my son to start walking and talking. Along with many other toys I made sure to buy him a pink, rubber ball. It didn't take long for us to start having a catch.

In the beginning he wasn't a good catcher or thrower. At first we stood close together and my throws were soft and right into his hands. Sometimes he would catch them and more often drop them. "That's it! You caught it!" or "Keep trying! You'll get it!" I often said. His throws weren't so straight and I often chased them down the driveway. I didn't mind.

As he grew older the pink, rubber ball was replaced by a baseball and glove. The oil we used to soften it hasn't changed. He recently asked, "Throw them high in the air, Dad." I do. When the ball stops at the top of its arc in the air and begins its descent I say, "Get under it. Get under it."

Aside from the "snap" of the ball hitting the glove, what seem to be echoes of "Nice catch," or "Good throw" can still be heard. I hope the smile on my face is as big as the one on his. The "conversation" hasn't changed, just the father and son. Now I've been on both ends. I wonder if the catches and throws speak volumes to him?

Dedications

To

Dad - Harold J. Theurer, a true gentleman
...and Anne, a devoted Mom who threw a
mean curve.

With Love:
To Lynne for the love and support
and Harold Eric, for continuing "the
catch". You make me proud.

Thanks to Hayden and Huffman - you never
stop teaching.

Harold Theurer, Jr.

For

My wife Jennifer and my children, Cassity,
Will & Greyson

Special thanks to:
Larry & Anita and Joe Huffman

For Johnny Lucas "Grand Daddy"

William Baxter Bledsoe

A very special thanks to:

Greyson Bledsoe, Harold Theurer III, Harold and Lynne Theurer, Johnnie Sue &
Isabelle Hawley, Bradd Porter, Joe Huffman (for all his encouragement), Frankie
Michaels, Baxter Johnson Bledsoe, Matthew Chandley, Larry & Anita Michaels
(thanks upon thanks), Mr. Rupert (in memory), Angela Cyrus, Mr. Garland Thayer (for
your leadership and example), Edward Mattie, T.L., Hollie and the FedexKinkos Team,
Rebecca Isabelle, Marilyn Buchannan and Wayne Dyer.

Thanks Again - Bill

Final Layout and Production:
Edward Mattie

Published by Column Hall Concepts, LLC.
P.O. Box 090263 Brooklyn, NY 11209
Text copyright ©2005 by Harold Theurer, Jr.
Illustrations ©2006 by William Baxter Bledsoe
All rights reserved

Requests for permission to make copies of any part of the work should be mailed to:
Column Hall Concepts, LLC
217-82nd Street, Brooklyn, NY 11209

Library of Congress Cataloging and Publication Data
Theurer, Jr., Harold
Hey Dad! Let's Have a Catch, by Harold Theurer, Jr.
Illustrated by William Baxter Bledsoe - 1st ed.

p. :ill: cm ISBN: 0-9786584-0-X

1. Playing Catch-non fiction 2. Brooklyn, NY - non fiction
1. Theurer, Harold Jr. 2. Bledsoe, William Baxter, ill.IV.Title

Second Edition
1098765432

Printed in the United States. The illustrations were rendered in watercolor wash over graphite on hot press
watercolor paper. The text was set in Times New Roman.